A KNIGHT ERRANT

RYAN SCOTT VAN ELLS

A KNIGHT ERRANT © 2024 Ryan Van Ells

Published by Graveside Press
graveside-press.com

All rights reserved.

This story is entirely a work of fiction. The names, characters, businesses, places, events and incidents portrayed in it are the work of the author's imagination or are used fictitiously. Any resemblance to actual persons, living or dead, events or localities is entirely coincidental. No part of this book may be reproduced or transmitted in any form or by any means, electronic or mechanical, except for the purpose of review and/or reference, without explicit permission in writing from the publishers.

Editing: Kelley York
Cover Design: Sleepy Fox Studio – sleepyfoxstudio.net
Interior Formatting: Sleepy Fox Studio – sleepyfoxstudio.net
Interior Art: Sleepy Fox Studio – sleepyfoxstudio.net

eBook 978-1-964952-35-2
Print (paperback) 978-1-964952-34-5

No part of this book has been created using Generative AI.

GRAVESIDE·PRESS

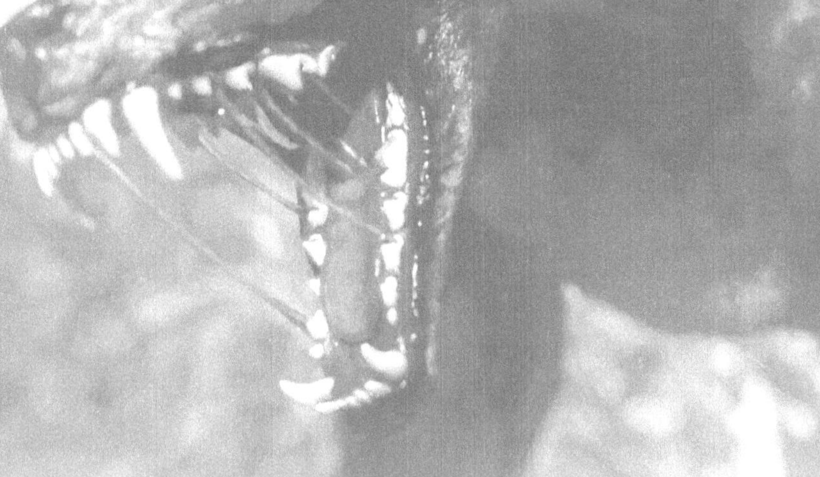

OLEN DID NOT LOOK like a knight. He was tall, yes, but thin and flimsy. His long limbs looked like they would snap if he picked up the heavy sword at his side. His gaunt face was more of the kind you would expect of a beggar than a knight errant.

Which is why Dagonet did not consider his offer seriously.

"You want to go after the werewolf?" Dagonet asked. "You have an army in that pack there?"

He did not. Olen hoped the night would hide the rips in his rain-soaked pack.

"No, sir." Olen tried to keep the quavering out of his voice. He hadn't eaten in some time; the work of a knight errant was seldom rewarding these days, and it made his voice weak. But Dagonet was likely to take this for youthful fear, so Olen kept his voice under control as best he could. "But I assure you, I can handle a werewolf on my own. I slew the Sea Serpent of Stirling." This was mostly true. Olen had stumbled upon the beast washed up on the beach and slit its belly open before it could realize it was not where it was meant to be.

"I heard that was Lancelot," Dagonet said.

Olen winced. Lancelot had indeed been present for the slaying of the beast and had even tried to make sure Olen got the credit. Neither the mayor nor the people believed him.

"No, that was I." Olen put a hand on the pommel of his sword, as if this would give him an air of credibility. Instead, the shift of weight threw him off-balance, and he took a step backward, nearly falling. Dagonet laughed.

"Listen, lad," Dagonet said when he stopped. "I like you, you're funny, so I'm going to give you a chance, but I'm not going to pay you up front—"

"But the flyer—" Olen started.

Dagonet held up a hand.

"Because, and don't take any offense to this, I don't think you can do it." The innkeeper shrugged. "It's not that you're not a capable boy, I'm sure you are. But I've seen stronger men than you try and fail. I paid them all for the trying, and haven't a penny left to spare for you."

Olen sighed and fingered his father's silver dagger on his hip.

"That's not to say that you won't be rewarded if you *do*

kill the beast. Bring back its head, and I'll be sure the whole of Graycott pitches in for your reward. And there won't be a maiden here not willing to toss a favor your way, eh?" Dagonet smacked him on the shoulder and laughed when Olen bent under the meaty man's weight. "But maybe sleep on it first. You have a bed for tonight?"

"Yes, sir," Olen said. "I've a friend in the village."

"Oh. Who's the friend?"

"Aleyn."

Dagonet frowned. "You sure you don't want a room? Lord knows we have the space." He gestured to the open inn behind him. A bright fire roared, warm and inviting, with only a handful of men around it.

"I'm sure. Aleyn is a friend, and we haven't seen each other in some time. It will be nice to catch up."

"If your mind is set," Dagonet said. "I don't know how long it's been since you've been to Graycott, boy, but let me give you a piece of advice." He leaned in so close that Olen could smell the beer on his breath. Dagonet's jovial smile disappeared, and the laugh lines on his face deepened into a grave expression. "Aleyn is not the man he used to be. Most folks here, well, they think he's of an odd sort. You won't get much help with your hunt if they know you're staying with him." He leaned back, his smile returning. "But that's just one old man's opinion. Just know the inn is open if you need it."

"Thank you, sir."

"You're welcome, lad."

Dagonet returned to the inn and closed the door behind him. The warm light went with it, leaving Olen in the dark and rain.

By the time Olen arrived at Aleyn's farm, the rain had let up, the stars were shining, and the smell of moist earth filled his nostrils. It might have been pleasant if not for the odor of cow shit mixed in there as well. He trudged up to the farmhouse, his boots squelching in the new mud, and knocked on the door. He had a sudden fear that everyone was asleep, leaving no one to invite him in. It would be another half an hour's walk back to the inn and they would be closed up by now. Why hadn't he just taken the innkeeper's offer?

Thankfully, there came a stirring from inside the house and a moment later, an elderly man, his face wearied with years of work and worry, answered the door.

"The hell you want?"

"Good evening, Alis," Olen said to Aleyn's father.

"Huh?" Alis squinted. "Oh, it's you. Aleyn's in the barn." He threw a hand in the direction of another large building a little way off from the house. Then he slammed the door before Olen could say anything further.

Olen shrugged the pack up higher on his shoulder and went to the barn.

The barn itself was a sturdy thing, made of thick stone walls and a thatched roof. It was a tall building that, during harvest time, would be filled to the brim with barley. Summer harvest was two months away, however, and the barn was empty save for a few piles of feeding hay. There wasn't a door, and Aleyn's sleeping form on the hay was clear from the outside.

Olen crept into the barn, trying not to disturb him. As he passed Aleyn's resting place, it burst to life. A flurry of hay exploded into the air, and Olen was grabbed around the neck and pulled into the pile. He collapsed on top of Aleyn, against his bare chest and enfolded in his arms. Olen blushed.

"Gotcha," Aleyn said, grinning.

"How did you know I was coming?"

"You never were as sneaky as you thought," Aleyn said. "Besides, I could hear old Alis's grumbling from up here."

Olen pulled against Aleyn's grip, to no avail. Aleyn had always been the stronger one. He leaned in and kissed

Olen.

"Aleyn!" Olen's face burned all over. "There's no door on this barn."

"The night is deep and dark, friend. And my father fell fast asleep as soon as you left his door."

"How do you know?"

"The old man always collapses into a coma when he's done putting his prick in Enid. Wonder you woke him up at all, actually."

Olen tried to pull away again.

"Don't be a nun, Olen," Aleyn said.

Olen felt the open door at his back like a hunter, feeling the wolf watching him from behind.

"Aleyn," he said as Aleyn's burning lips found his neck. Then, "Aleyn…" again, his voice trailing off as Aleyn's lips sent a tingle of pleasure shivering from his neck through his spine. His hairs stood up on their tips, erect with sensation. Like a hunger-striking monk suddenly confronted with his mother's steak pie, Olen knew this was what he'd been missing in the last year.

They made love in the hay.

Olen and Aleyn lay beside each other, chests heaving. Straw stuck to their sweat-slicked bodies.

"I missed you," Aleyn said.

Olen laughed.

"You missed fucking."

"That too. But I also missed you."

"I don't believe it," Olen said. "You'd have all the village if you were able."

"I'd only have you." Aleyn turned onto his side to gaze down at him.

"You don't mean that."

"I do," Aleyn said with a sternness in his voice that almost made Olen believe it was true. "You should live here."

Olen laughed again.

"I mean it," Aleyn continued. "Live in Graycott. You could work at the inn and save. My parents aren't long for this world. When they die, you can come stay with me at the farm."

Olen thought about it more sincerely than he intended. He thought about the shame of being a failed knight errant without a homestead, forced to work for pennies and a room. About how dull the day-to-day labor of a farmer would be. About how he and Aleyn, if anyone were to discover them, would be driven out of town—or worse.

And about how damn much he would love a calm life by Aleyn's side…if only it could work.

"You only want me because I'm not at your beck and call," Olen said after a moment. "If I were here every day, you'd get bored." Aleyn opened his mouth to protest, but Olen cut him off. "And can you imagine me as a *farmer*? I'm a knight. I travel. I perform feats. A farmer's life is not for me."

"It's not so bad," Aleyn said. He was playing with a piece of straw between his fingers. "And what kind of knight are you, anyway? What feats have you done that have not been claimed by another? What wealth and honor have you gained? I hear even your land has been taken by another. Now, nothing you gain is your own. Nothing you have ever done has earned their respect and nothing ever will. Why not give it up?"

Olen wanted to yell. He wanted to tell Aleyn that everything he said was true and that was exactly why he couldn't stop. If he quit now, every person who never believed in his deeds, every person who denied him his payment, and every person who stole his land would be proven right.

But Aleyn had heard all of that before. They had this conversation every year, and he was tired of it.

"I'm going after the werewolf," Olen said.

Aleyn sat up straight. "Why the hell would you want to do that?"

"What do you mean? It's a monster and I'm a knight. It's kind of what we do."

"It's what other knights do, you mean," Aleyn said. "Not you."

Olen laughed. "I've killed monsters before. This is no different. Besides, the award is good, if that fat innkeeper can afford it."

Aleyn was silent.

"You don't think I should," Olen said.

"I don't want you to get hurt."

"It's a risk of the job; you knew this when we met. What changed?"

"Nothing," Aleyn said. "I just care about you more now. I can't stand the thought of you getting hurt."

"You don't think I can do it." Olen's heart hollowed out, and he was suddenly aware of his nudity. He stood up and began to dress. "Do you even believe me when I tell you what I've done? Do you think I'm an actual knight, or are you just like everyone else?"

"It's not that," Aleyn said.

"Then what is it?"

"Why do you have to?"

"Because I'm a knight and it's killing people," Olen said.

He sat down next to Aleyn. "Because I need to prove I can do this." With the words spoken, the anger flushed out of Olen like he had pulled the stopper holding it in.

"Please don't," Aleyn murmured. He didn't look up, but Olen could see he was crying. Olen pulled him close.

"It will be alright," he said. "I'm going to be okay."

They held each other through the night.

When Olen awoke, Aleyn was nowhere to be found. The full moon was due the next night, so Olen didn't wait to look for him. Instead, he headed out alone.

"That's where I found my boy," Farmer Bisir said, pointing to a patch of earth in his field. The sheep farmer had been the last person to see the werewolf, according to Dagonet. "That's where my Jerem was. At least, the parts I could recognize." He was crying. Olen put a hand on his shoulder and waited for the man to stop.

"Where did it go?"

"Over there." Bisir pointed to the dense woods that edged the field. "No man with any sense goes into those woods."

Olen nodded. He knew this to be true about Graycott;

it was common knowledge that the Black Woods held all manner of dangerous and savage creatures, but that didn't mean Graycott's residents knew anything beyond bedtime stories about them.

One summer, the blacksmith swore a troll had appeared and stole his forge hammer. This was false. Trolls lived in the caves of high mountainous regions, not in the flat forests of the south. Not to mention they had no interest in forge craft; whatever weapons they used were scavenged from the poor fools who stumbled across them after missing their obnoxious scent. And when it was revealed that the tanner was the one to have taken it, he in turn swore that a fairie had appeared from the woods and tricked him into stealing it. No one wanted to risk the wrath of a fairie who wanted a forge hammer, so the tanner was allowed to keep it, and the blacksmith was purchased a new one from the village coffers.

The one thing different about the werewolf, however, was that it was seen by many of the villagers. A shopkeeper had seen it creeping at the edge of town. The innkeeper had watched it tear the head off of one of Farmer Bisir's sheep. And Farmer Bisir himself had seen it loping through his fields after murdering his son.

"I shan't go any further," Farmer Bisir said, his voice trembling.

"I wouldn't expect you to," Olen said. The woods were dense and dark. Even at midday, the light barely pierced the thick overgrowth of trees. At the treeline, brambles and vines crept outward, hinting at the future stumbling blocks within.

"You shouldn't either."

"I must."

"Think of Aleyn."

Olen looked at the old man, the surprise apparent on his face.

"I just know the boy cares for you," Bisir continued, averting his gaze. "I know what it feels like to lose someone you care about."

Olen, feeling a sudden surge of confidence much unlike him, strode forward and put a hand on the man's shoulder. "And I can't allow anyone else to feel that pain."

The man did not respond. He met Olen's gaze with tear-filled eyes and nodded.

Once beyond the first line of trees, Olen found the forest brighter than he expected. Trickles of sunlight lit the woods, and he was able to find what he was looking for rather quickly—a broken branch here, a tuft of wolf-like fur there, and dried wolf prints in the mud of a creek.

The paw print was larger than any wolf's he'd ever seen. In fact, it would have been large even for a bear. He was no match for whatever made this track, werewolf or not. One of the common misconceptions the villagers had about werewolves was that they only transformed on a full moon. It was true that a werewolf would be at its full strength under a full moon, but the light of *any* moon was enough to bring about the transformation. Olen wanted to turn around. But the thought of returning to Jerem's father empty-handed and the strong sun, now glaring down at this break in the trees, encouraged him forward.

The tracks, sparse but frequent enough to follow, led Olen down the bank of the creek until it became a stream, and then eventually a waterfall. Not a big one; it was slightly taller than Olen, but to the north the hill it rested on grew taller still. Looking there, Olen spotted a patched-together shield of bramble and vines that would appear to someone with less experience as just another untraversable path in the Black Woods, but to Olen's trained eyes, he recognized it was not quite right. When he got closer, he saw why.

The patch was man made and weaved into the forest to appear like a piece of brush. But it was not and could be easily moved. Olen gripped it, thankful for his thick leather gloves preventing the thorns from piercing his skin, and yanked the brush away piece by piece to reveal the large cave entrance that reminded him uncomfortably of a troll's den.

It was further down from the mountains than Olen had ever seen one before, yet this was, unmistakably, a troll cave. Not the cave of a large troll. They usually grew to about ten-foot tall and their bodies were a ton of dense, rock-like flesh. This cave was only eight feet tall at best, a tight fit for a below-average troll. But it carried all the telltale signs: deer and wolf bones intermixed in piles and covered in square tooth marks, a massive fire pit too deep in the cave for proper ventilation, and a large mat of leaves and branches that couldn't have been much more comfortable than the ground.

The biggest clue, though, was the stench of acidic sweat—an odor that seeped into the ground and held there for months if the troll stayed put for more than an hour. It's what made them so easy to track. The scent was weaker than Olen would expect. If this were a troll cave, it hadn't been home in the last several months.

Deeper inside, Olen discovered why. The troll's bones were piled haphazardly where it had fallen.

Even a small troll like this was capable of taking on more than a handful of well-armed men at a time, especially in its own home. And, given its weight, Olen doubted anyone had dragged the creature inside for dinner.

Whatever felled a cave troll was not something to be

handled lightly. Deeper still in the cave, several smaller sleeping mats were laid out. More bones—sheep and deer mostly, though a few human skulls as well—were piled in corners. Tufts of fur similar to those in the forest had caught on the walls.

Where the cave's inhabitant was now, he could not be sure, but there was no doubt in Olen's mind. Whatever it had been home to previously was irrelevant.

This was a werewolf den.

Light faded quickly once the sun descended below the tree line. It was hard for Olen to know whether or not night had come. He hurried through the underbrush, counting on shadowy forms that resembled earlier landmarks, and cursed himself for being so careless with time. He'd been so focused on finding the beast that he'd forgotten the basics. One of the first things his father taught him about hunting: always know the sun and how far you are from home. Olen fingered his father's dagger at his side. It was a good luck charm that had gotten him through many a tough spot; he would need it here.

Eventually, through crafty rangership and pure dumb

luck, Olen crossed the tree line back into the fields outside Graycott just after the sun had set. He put his hands on his knees and caught his breath. He should've brought his damn horse.

When Olen stood straight again, night had fully taken over, and he knew something was wrong.

An uncanny silence had fallen over the landscape along with the darkness: no chirp of crickets, no rabbits in the underbrush, not even the bleating of sheep in the nearby field. It was the silence of everything hiding in fear.

Olen scanned the trees; there was no movement he could discern in the darkness.

The hair on the back of Olen's neck crept up. He swung around, despite himself, to the empty field behind him. Still, his neck tingled as though the eyes of a predator were running up and down it.

By the time he turned back around, it was too late.

A blur of fur and jagged claws came out of the brush and were on top of Olen before he knew it. He fell. His calf roared in fiery agony. Olen twisted around and kicked out blindly toward the pain with his good leg. He connected with flesh that gave way under his boot. The beast yelped.

Olen jumped to his feet and unsheathed his sword. Deep claw marks had gouged through his pants and into his calf. Blood gushed. Not great, but better than a bite. Bites were infectious. Olen tried to put weight on the leg. He clenched his jaw as pain shot up through him, but the limb held.

The wolf growled menacingly where it hunched on all fours. One injured eye was half-shut and blinking rapidly. Olen was never more grateful for investing in thick boots.

He raised his sword and pointed it at the beast.

"Come on."

The wolf stood on its hind legs with preternatural ease. It let loose a wild howl, deeper and more bone-chilling than any wolf Olen had heard before. Its face was more beast than man; thick, yellowed fangs protruded from a snarling snout. Coarse black fur clung tight to sinewy muscles.

Then it came. It loped forward on its back legs. Olen had only a moment to react.

He pointed his blade down, then swung upward in a quick, violent motion. The wolf dodged right at the last moment and the blade only nicked the edge of a foreleg. The wolf growled as it tumbled out of range. The blade's momentum swung up. Olen braced hard and brought it back to neutral. His pulse pounded in his ears. He was getting light-headed from blood loss. He needed to end this quickly.

But there was no time to think. The wolf came at him

again on all fours. Olen leaped back as claws ricocheted off his breastplate and his weight came down on his bad leg. It gave. He fell on his ass. His sword dropped beside him an inch out of reach. The wolf took the opportunity and pounced, mouth open and hungry. Olen whipped his father's dagger from its hip sheath and thrust it forward, blindly hoping to put something sharp between him and the werewolf. It scraped the wolf's shoulder as its head came down.

The beast yelped and reared back. It groped its paw to its injured shoulder in a very human movement.

In that moment, Olen grabbed his sword and swung in a wide arc. The blade connected, severing the wolf's clawed hand. Its scream, too, sounded eerily human at its core.

The shoulder the wolf was protecting was already hairless and pink around the dagger wound. It dashed toward the forest, slowing each step of the way, and leaving its severed wolf hand behind. Olen wanted to follow. He made to get up, but blood loss and the associated dizziness were too much.

The last thing he thought before he lost consciousness was that he should have told Aleyn where he was going.

Olen woke in blurry spurts: sensations of movement, of being carried, of being bandaged. When he came to, sunlight poured into his eyes. He lifted a hand to block it out.

"Damn the light," he muttered. Olen raised himself to a sitting position. He was in Aleyn's barn again, atop a pile of blood-soaked hay. Light flowed in from the doorway. The sun was still low enough to aim itself straight into the barn and Olen's face.

"Thank the gods," Aleyn said. He stepped from the darkness in the back of the barn. His eyes were red, his face puffy. Had he been crying?

Aleyn marched forward and pulled him into a firm hug. What little breath that remained in Olen went out of him.

"I was so worried about you," Aleyn said. His hands gripped Olen's back as if to keep him in this plane of existence by pure physical strength alone. Then, just as suddenly, Aleyn released the hug, put Olen's face between his hands, and looked him in the eyes.

"How could you be so *stupid*?" he asked, though it didn't sound like a question he actually expected an answer to.

"Excuse me?" Olen said after he caught his breath.

"Going out to the woods alone at night, knowing what's out there," Aleyn continued as if Olen hadn't spoken. He dropped his hands and stood. "Did you think you could win?"

"Why do you say it like that?"

Aleyn looked at him as though just now aware that Olen was taking part in this conversation. "Like *what*?"

"Like you don't think I can do it. Not anyone. Not another knight. *Me*."

"That's not what I meant."

"Do you think Lancelot could do it?"

"Olen…"

"Or Gawain?"

"Olen."

"I *did* win, so you're aware. It didn't get to town, it didn't hurt anyone, and now I know—"

"Olen, I can't lose you!" There were fresh tears in Aleyn's eyes. "You passed out. You were nearly dead from blood loss and who knows what would have happened if that thing came back to finish the job? Look at yourself. Look at your leg. If I hadn't been there…gods know." He slumped to the floor, his hands over his face.

In his anger, Olen had forgotten about his calf. It was wrapped in a fresh bandage, marred by only a few spots of blood compared to the soaked hay pile beneath him. He inferred that it'd been changed several times. Olen tested the leg. A stab of pain went through it, but he could stand.

He limped the few steps over to Aleyn and sat down beside him, then waited for the sobbing to cease.

"I'm going to have to go after it again," Olen said softly.

Aleyn looked up at him, his face screwed up in a way that suggested he was torn between crying more and yelling.

Olen continued. "You're right. It's not dead. And with tonight being a full moon, it will be stronger, more dangerous, and probably mad as all the hells. It could—no, it *will* hurt someone."

"But why you?" Aleyn asked, almost under his breath, as if he weren't speaking to Olen at all.

"Because I'm the one who can."

"But you can't, not this."

Olen flinched at the reproach but did not respond. He did not feel like going in circles anymore. They sat in silence for a long moment.

"I care for you, you know," Olen finally said.

Aleyn nodded to himself. He stood as if to leave.

"Stay?" Olen asked. Aleyn paused. "It's still early; I don't have to leave until later. I could use this."

Aleyn leaned down and kissed him; it was tender, like a kiss for a dying lover that he did not want to forget. "I care for you too," Aleyn said when they broke. "That's why I can't watch you do this to yourself."

He left.

Olen sat in the rising sunlight, surrounded by his own blood. He wondered how much more of it he would see before this was over.

No inhabitant of Graycott would cross into the forest with Olen, so he returned alone. He believed the cave was where the werewolf would go to transform, and he hoped to arrive early and catch it before it began, but his new limp slowed him, and the woods proved to be more confusing in the low light than he remembered. He found himself turned around as soon as he lost sight of the tree line and did not arrive at the cave until well after the moon rose.

Olen briefly considered leaving to head off the werewolf at the village but dismissed the idea. He did not know where it would be tonight, and even if it were to enter Graycott, he had no ability to know where in Graycott it would show up. Besides, even with the moon full and bright, the forest was dark and confusing. Olen doubted he could make his way back to the village without getting turned around. If he wandered aimlessly in the woods, all he'd succeed in doing was getting lost, and then more people would get hurt. At least this way, he was sure to meet it. And, if it were not, he could at least return to Graycott with better vision in the morning.

So, Olen sat on a rock outside the cave and waited. And waited. His armor, not normally restricting, was heavy and his back labored under the extra weight. His calf throbbed. He'd eaten little during his time in Graycott and even less in the days before. Sweat dripped down his forehead. He roughly wiped it away. It was too early for this kind of exhaustion. A breeze swept through the woods, its cool brush on his face welcome. When the rustle of leaves ceased, there was not a sound. It was an eerie quiet, without even the hoot of an owl to hint at life.

Just as the thought came to Olen's mind, an echoing howl came from inside the cave. Olen's skin prickled. The moon was nearly down, and the sky was about to lighten.

The werewolf had been inside the cave the entire time.

He turned around to face the entrance, a hand on the hilt of his sword. Though the sky was at the tipping point of lightening, the cave itself was pitch black. There was no way of telling where in the dark the sharp teeth of the werewolf were. Olen felt himself being watched. He strained to listen. Every brush of wind felt like the deep breath of the beast.

Olen took a step back, his armor clanking in his ears and echoing through the night air. He swallowed hard.

He imagined the swiping of a bear-sized claw that felled a seven-foot cave troll and was all too aware of the fact that he was alone. He wanted nothing more than to plunge himself into the thick forest behind him, to disappear into the bramble and brush and flee to Graycott.

But he could not. The unknown knight errant, the country knight without a shred of land to his name anymore, who had won no ladies' favors, felled no beasts on his own, and succeeded in no quests, running away from a bounty he vowed to himself to earn? There was no Lancelot to be given credit for his work this time. There was no chance to blame his victory on. He would either return to Graycott with the head of the werewolf, or not return at all.

Olen lit a torch.

He was a knight and knights, as a rule, weren't quiet. But Olen was not just a knight. He was a country knight, a knight who grew up on the farm and hunted in the woods, a knight who had experience tracking. In reality, he was more hunter than knight. And in the werewolf's cave, he aimed to prove it.

His footsteps were soft on the earth, his armor made no clanging sound you would expect of a knight, and his breath was shallow and soft. No man would hear his approach. Hell, no bird would either. Which is why, when he made his way to the back area of the cave, the werewolves had made no notice of him.

Werewolves, plural.

Olen held back a curse.

Of course there had to be more than one. That explained the multiple cots at least, but it sure made his job a hell of a lot harder. He thought briefly of killing only one, but he dismissed the idea immediately. If he made an attempt on one, the others would spring into action beside their comrade. Not to mention the fact that the village's problems would only continue, and he would be the knight who killed the wrong werewolf.

The problem then became how to engage with the pack. Olen had prepared for only one werewolf, not seven. None of them seemed to have noticed him. They were staring away, into darkness, distracted. He could maybe get a strike in on one before the others turned on him, but then he was in dire straits.

As Olen pondered this, the werewolves convulsed. He looked on in terror as the monsters' hair retracted, their muscles curled into themselves, and their massive bodies shrunk. It was like watching a mouse be trampled under a horse's hoof. But, instead of a flat mouse pancake, there were men. Seven naked, shivering men curled in on themselves in pain.

One of whom was Aleyn.

Olen could not move. When the werewolves changed, his plan had as well—into slaying the werewolves while in their human form as they recovered from their transformation. While not the most honorable, it was the only way to ensure that he got all the wolves and, as much as he wanted the honor of beating a werewolf in single combat, he would have to hope the village folks would appreciate the gesture, anyway. But when Olen recognized Aleyn's face where the wolf's head had been a minute before, all his planning faded.

"You never were as sneaky as you thought," Aleyn called.

"Aleyn..."

"Olen." Aleyn's eyes darted to him. "What are you doing here?"

"I could ask you the same question."

Aleyn grimaced, yet he responded with his trademark wit. "I asked you first."

Olen gestured with his sword still drawn. "Hunting werewolves." To call himself dumbfounded would be an understatement. Aghast, perhaps. Whatever Olen felt, his blood was coursing through him at a remarkable speed.

"I see."

The other men had gotten to their feet and steadily surrounded Olen, taking flank positions. One who wore a scar on his shoulder and was missing a hand sneered. They were unarmed and nude, but they positioned themselves like a pack of predators. Even with his armor and sword, Olen doubted if he could handle all of them if they came at him.

"I guess you found what you were looking for," Aleyn continued. His voice was soft now. Somber. "You have your head to bring back to Graycott."

Olen felt a million things—wanted to *say* a million things. But mostly he was angry. He wanted to yell at Aleyn, to scream at him for holding back such an important secret from him. He wanted to yell at himself for never realizing. He wanted to rip the other men apart limb from limb, to punish them for scaring those innocent villagers and for killing Jerem; and he wanted to laugh hysterically because it was so *perfect* that Aleyn, who despised everything and everyone in Graycott, was the one behind it all. Anger and fear and sadness and other emotions he couldn't name rushed over him and all he could say was, "How?"

Aleyn smirked that irritable, one-sided smirk. "The same as anyone else."

"Who..." Olen was about to say *who are these men*, but stopped, feeling embarrassed. But Aleyn understood.

"I was confused at first, too," Aleyn said. "About why

I was bitten but not eaten, about why I was saved. But Ceargan explained it all to me. That they are like me. Like you. Like us."

"I am not like you—not like that."

"No, Olen. Like *us*." Aleyn stepped forward, well within the range of Olen's blade. Olen did not raise it. He should have been afraid, but he wasn't. Aleyn put his hand in Olen's.

Like us, Olen thought. He looked around at the naked men in the cavern. They were oddly silent, looking to Aleyn for instruction.

"Look at them, Olen," Aleyn said. "They are free. *We* are free here."

"But you're hurting people."

"Only those who deserve it." Aleyn scowled. "Jerem saw us, Olen. Saw us together as men in the forest. He threatened to kill us. It was self-defense. Besides, what good would killing us do, anyway?" The men in the cave shifted at the word *kill*. They were afraid. Good. "Bring back the head of one, hell, *seven* werewolves to Graycott and...what? You think they'll worship you? Ha." He barked a short laugh. "You think they'll even respect you? You think they won't call you a coward for slaying the beasts in human form instead of while the moon is high? No. No, they will never give you the respect you deserve,

Olen. You know why? Because they sense it on you. They smell your difference. No matter what you do, no matter how brave or perfect or chivalrous you are, you will never be Lancelot. You'll forever be Olen the undeserving, a knight without land or fame."

While Aleyn spoke, Olen noticed the men shifting around him, moving in just another step closer every time they thought Olen was distracted by Aleyn's words. The man without the hand had spread further from his fellows and stood behind Olen and likely thought himself invisible. Olen shifted his weight off his bad leg and kept his ears trained on the man's movements.

"What would you have me do?" Olen asked. "Join you? Ravage the countryside? Murder and steal and spread terror because a few shun me?"

"Not a few," Aleyn spat. "All."

Olen swallowed. This felt close to the conversations they'd had in their younger years, when righteous fury emanated from them. Only, back then, Olen had been speaking in theory. Aleyn had been serious. More serious than Olen ever knew, he now realized.. And, just as he had in those conversations, Olen had a nagging suspicion in his soul that Aleyn was right. For all his hopes, there was no guarantee that the head of this werewolf would be the one that brought him his rightful glory.

Just then, the man behind Olen sprang forward to grab him from behind. Olen spun in a circle, bringing a closed, armored fist cracking against the man's cheek. He felt a tooth loosen beneath his knuckles. The man collapsed onto the ground, spitting blood. Olen didn't stop to look. He continued his spin into a full circle, switching his sword hand and shifting the blade into a ready position. Could a fully armored knight take on seven—well, six—naked men and survive? He was about to find out. The other men made their first steps to jump forward.

"Wait!"

The men stopped at Aleyn's command. Olen kept himself tense.

"That was dumb," Aleyn said, both to Olen and the man on the floor. "I apologize. Emotions are high. We all just want to protect our own."

From the way Aleyn looked at him, Olen realized that Aleyn considered him as one of Aleyn's own. There was a twinge of remorse in Olen's heart, and then Aleyn, who had distanced himself during his pacing monologue, stepped forward again, and this time Olen did not restrain himself. He readied the blade to swing. Aleyn looked hurt.

"You wouldn't," he said.

"Try me."

Aleyn flinched. He believed him. The cocky smirk was wiped off his face. Olen used to love that damn smirk.

"I love you," Aleyn said. The words punched Olen in the gut and stole his breath. "We can be together."

For a second, Olen was mystified. Aleyn, tall and farm-muscled and blonde, was telling him he loved him. Just as he had in the barn, and every other night they had ever laid together. He was being offered a place at Aleyn's side. He would be free of the trappings of a knight, to do as and who he pleased.

Gods, it was *tempting*.

He thought of all the world who gave him nothing for all he offered and considered what it would be like to turn the tables on it.

And he thought of his legacy, to be known forever as a failed knight who died on his only quest alone.

Olen wanted nothing more than for the voice of a villager to come from the cave entrance, for someone or something to save him from having to make this choice.

Nothing did.

He let out the breath he'd been holding, sheathed his sword, and approached Aleyn. As they came close, he grabbed the back of Aleyn's head and drew him into a kiss, long and deep and hard, as if they were alone in the barn and it was Olen's last night in Graycott before departing for Gods knew how long—perhaps the last time they'd ever get to do so. Aleyn fell into the kiss.

A kiss just long and distracting enough for Olen to draw his father's dagger from his belt and shove it into Aleyn's stomach.

Even a small amount of silver would kill a werewolf if given enough time. Olen's problem was that the silver content of the dagger was a *very* small amount.

Aleyn stepped back and let loose a bestial howl of furious agony that echoed off the cave walls. It was the sound of a rabid dog fighting over a scrap of meat, not that of his former lover. Something in it triggered a primordial fight-or-flight response within Olen. His hairs stood on end, and he wanted nothing more than to run. He planted his feet. His calf twinged.

With a centering breath, Olen shifted to a fighting posture, careful to keep all the werewolves in view, and readied his sword at Aleyn.

"I love you too," he said, his voice resigned, "but I can't let anyone else suffer at your hands."

Aleyn spat. His eyes narrowed. Whatever softness had been on his face was gone. "You're not doing this for anyone else," he said. "You're doing it for your own damn pride."

Olen did not have a chance to respond. Aleyn leaped at

him, teeth bared and snarling, an arm outstretched with still clawed fingers ready to slash. Even outside of his bestial form, wounded and poisoned, Aleyn was stronger and faster than a normal man.

Olen tried to sidestep, but his calf protested, and his balance went wrong. He was too slow to avoid the worst of it. Warm pain shot through Olen's neck as Aleyn's claws sliced through skin and muscle. Olen hissed and reached instinctively to cover the wound but was stopped as he was grabbed from behind. His neck bloomed in sharp agony as the assailant bit down into the open wound. Olen screamed. He elbowed blindly, catching his attacker in the nose. They did not relent.

"Back off," yelled Aleyn. "He's mine!" Olen thought he saw genuine panic in Aleyn's eyes. Then it was gone, replaced by animal indifference.

The one-handed man released Olen's neck, leaving behind a burning pain throbbing there. He clutched at the wound.

The werewolves had closed on Olen faster than he could have expected. They encircled him, mere steps away. If Aleyn hadn't stopped them, Olen would be under a dog pile right now.

The pack backed away, making room for Aleyn to approach again. Olen lifted his sword and tried to keep the tip aimed at Olen. It wavered with each throb of pain in his neck. The hilt was heavy in his grip, and he needed both hands to hold the sword steady. It felt like there was sludge in his blood being pushed through with each heartbeat. Was this the werewolf's poison? If he didn't end this soon, he would not make it.

As Aleyn took another step, Olen's injured leg buckled, and he fell to one knee. He leaned the sword against his leg and raised a hand to Aleyn.

"Wait," Olen said. Blood and sweat slicked his body. He forced his breathing into ragged gasps. If there was one thing Aleyn believed in, it was Olen's weakness. Aleyn strode up to him. He stood above him and sneered down. His veins were a sickening black, spread out from where the dagger still protruded from his stomach.

"I did love you," Aleyn said, "but you made your choice." He drew back a leg as if to kick Olen. But the poison in Aleyn's blood had blurred his perception and made him slow. As Aleyn had been approaching, Olen had gathered loose dirt from the cave floor. He now tossed a fistful of it into Aleyn's eyes. Aleyn snarled out in rage and pawed at his face.

"Dir—"

Olen didn't let him finish. He rose and, with a single fluid motion, wrenched the dagger from Aleyn's stomach and drove it back into the werewolf's heart. Aleyn stumbled back, his face twisted with surprise and fury. There was nothing left in his eyes of the man Olen had spent the night in the barn with. There didn't seem to be much man left in Aleyn at all. He was pure animal rage.

Then Aleyn's eyes were wide with realization and terror. He collapsed, dead, on the cave floor.

Olen turned to face the rest of the werewolves, chest heaving, ready to fall under their attack.

They were frozen still. In fact, they recoiled at his gaze. These men would have followed Aleyn to the end of the earth and, from their perspective, just had. Without his leadership, they had nowhere to turn. Olen pitied them. But pity or not, they were still werewolves, and Olen was a knight.

Before he could go for his sword, a voice came from the entrance of the cave.

"In here! I think he's in here!"

It was Farmer Bisir. He must have mustered the courage to enter the forest after all. More voices came from behind him, bouncing off the cave walls. With the echoes, it was impossible to tell how many followed. It could be the whole village for all Olen knew.

"Hello?" Bisir shouted.

Footsteps grew louder with the approaching

townspeople. Olen whipped around and saw the pack running deeper into the darkness of the cave. In a moment, they disappeared from view.

"Here," Olen yelled back, too tired to pursue.

The villagers—there were only four, not the whole village as Olen had thought earlier— rushed in beside him.

"You're alive," Bisir said and then saw Aleyn on the floor. "And successful?"

"In a sense," Olen said, then followed up with, "the werewolf is dead," before anyone could ask him what he meant. The villagers looked at him with some mixture of disbelief, appreciation, and awe.

"It was Aleyn all along." Bisir shook his head.

Olen only nodded, but it seemed enough for Bisir. He regarded Olen with what Olen thought was pity.

"Can you walk?" Bisir asked.

"I can manage."

One of the villagers grabbed Olen's sword and, before Olen could scream *no*, swung it through Aleyn's neck.

Olen lunged for the villager, ignoring the pain in his leg, and grabbed him by the shirt.

"Who the fuck do you think you are?!" Rage boiled over inside him. If he'd been holding his sword, this man, this stranger, would be dead: beheaded alongside Aleyn.

The villager looked at him, mouth agape, unable to

form words. Tears stung Olen's eyes.

Then Bisir's hand was on his shoulder. He looked up at the old farmer. Bisir's face was compassionate, empathetic even, but stern. The old man shook his head. Olen understood. He did not want to understand. He did not want to care. But he did. He let go of the man's shirt and turned away to wipe the tears from his eyes.

"Stealing a knight's kill with his own sword," Bisir roared at the villager, "you are a fool indeed."

The man sputtered nonsense.

"Return his blade and speak nothing of being the one to chop the wolf's head and maybe the knight'll forgive you. What say you, sir knight?"

Olen nodded. He could say nothing more. Not without choking on the lump in his throat.

"Good enough," Bisir said. "Let's take the beast back and claim your reward."

Olen picked up Aleyn's body and took a trembling step. Bisir reached out a hand to support him, but Olen shrugged it off. Aleyn had carried him back alone. The least he could do was return the favor. With a renewed strength that ought to have been impossible, Olen carried Aleyn outside. The wound on his neck pulsed, but he ignored it. A problem to be dealt with later.

They left the cave. The villagers laughed and clapped

Olen on the back. They sang victorious battle songs. They called him Sir Knight. Olen held his head high and headed back to Graycott, Aleyn in his arms, limping all the way.

ABOUT THE AUTHOR

Ryan Van Ells (he/him) is a queer lawyer and author of dark fiction from Milwaukee, WI. His work has appeared, or is forthcoming, on Creepy Podcast, in October Screams and Drabbledark III. When not writing, Ryan can be found hunting for the best dark roast in the Midwest. You can visit him at ryanvanellsauthor.wordpress.com.